The Adventures of Papa Lemon's Little Wanderers
Book 2
The Dangerous Escape From Slavery

written by Lehman Riley
edited by Megan Austin
illustrated by Joshua Wallace

www.papalemonedu.com

Text copyright © 2005, by Lehman Riley.
Illustrations by Joshua Wallace.
All rights reserved to Matter of Africa America Time Corporation®
including the right of reproduction in whole or in part in any form.
Printed in the United States of America.
Lehman Riley/Matter of Africa America Time Corporation®
P.O. Box 11535
Minneapolis, MN 55411
Library of Congress Catalog Card No. 2005929138
ISBN 0-9760523-1-8

Excitement filled the air one warm Sunday afternoon. All of the Little Wanderers and their parents had arrived at Papa Lemon and Mama Sarah's house, ready for a big picnic in a far away park. Baby Buck could be heard anxiously shouting out, "Can we go now?"

His mother patiently replied, "No, Baby Buck, you know we have to wait for your aunt Kay."

Baby Buck thought for a moment. "Is she the one that always takes pictures of everybody?"

"Yes," answered his mother, "she is and you should be happy that she does. She can go way back in our family history with the pictures she has taken. When she gets here, I want you to give her a great big hug and tell her you're glad to see her."

Looking at his shoes, Baby Buck answered, "I will, Mom."

Just as Baby Buck made his promise, Aunt Kay pulled into the driveway and got out of her car with her trusty camera in hand. "Hi, everybody!" she shouted, waving both hands. "Oh, look at you darling kids! Come here so I can take a picture of all of you in a group."

Baby Buck and his mom exchanged knowing smiles.

"Okay," directed Kay, " I want Kaya and Carlos to stand in the back—you two are the tallest… AJ and Nikki, get on your knees and Baby Buck, sit in the front." Click, click went the camera. "Beautiful," she smiled. "Thank you!"

The kids rushed to Aunt Kay asking her for copies of the pictures. "I'll give all of you copies," she promised. Then she held up a warning finger and said, "But you must take care of them."

"We will!" the children nodded excitedly.

Clutching her camera, Aunt Kay headed off in the direction of the grown-ups. Soon Papa Lemon's voice could be heard saying, "Let's get going!"

The kids rushed over to Papa Lemon's car. "We want to ride with you," they said.

"It's okay with me if it's okay with your parents." He raised one eyebrow.

"They said we could!" informed Nikki.

"I get to sit next to the window!" AJ announced.

Carlos quickly followed suit. "I get the other one!"

"I'm not sitting in the middle!" whined a put-out Baby Buck.

"Too bad," Carlos taunted. "You didn't call a window seat. You will have to ride in the middle or go with your mom!"

Mama Sarah spoke up and asked Baby Buck if he wanted to ride in the front with her and Papa Lemon. Kaya studied her fingernails and said quietly, "I wanted to ride in front with you."

Baby Buck told Kaya, "Go ahead, I'll stay in back."

Kaya smiled and settled into the seat between Papa Lemon and Mama Sarah.

No sooner had the car warmed up than the questions began. "Why are we going to a park so far away?" AJ asked.

Papa Lemon gently answered, "My family used to come to this park when we had our family picnics. I was just a little boy when I first came here."

"When was that?" asked Nikki.

"Oh, that was in the early 1900's," he answered.

"WOW! That long ago?" Carlos asked, clearly in disbelief.

Papa Lemon and Mama Sarah exchanged chuckles. "Yep, that was a long time ago," agreed Mama Sarah.

"When were you born?" Nikki pressed.

"1896," Papa Lemon answered.

"OH MAN!" the kids exclaimed. They mumbled something about not even having television back then.

"Hey, look! It's the park!" Kaya shouted.

Baby Buck joined the excitement. "Let's play tag when we get out! Carlos is IT!"

"Before you kids go running off, I want to tell you about this park," interrupted Papa Lemon. "This is more than a park. This is where the slaves hid out when they ran from their slave masters. We come here to remember what those people went through. Some made it, but some died here waiting in these cold caves for a sign to come out," he explained gravely.

"Do you think there are skeletons in there?" asked wide-eyed AJ as he inched closer to Baby Buck.

"Maybe," answered Papa Lemon, "along with things that people dropped along the way. If those walls could talk I'm sure there would be some very sad stories." His voice had grown soft. Mama Sarah reached over and patted his hand gently. With that, the kids filed out of the car one at a time.

"I've heard stories like that before," announced Nikki, "about slaves running for freedom. I don't feel like playing tag anymore. Why don't we go check out the cave?"

"That sounds dangerous," AJ said nervously. "We didn't ask our parents…"

"Stop being a chicken," taunted Baby Buck. "We're just going to look!"

Carlos pointed at something. "I see a cave over there—follow me!"

As they ran, Nikki said breathlessly, "I wonder what we'll find."

"There's nothing in there," Carlos assured her. "That was so long ago."

They reached the mouth of the cave. AJ started to protest, but he was quickly informed that he was welcome to return to the car if he was too scared; the group was going in. One by one they entered the cave. Hesitant, AJ took a

deep breath and followed the rest of the gang.

Nikki took charge. "Now, everyone stick together!" she enforced. "That means no running ahead of us, Baby Buck," she said, raising her eyebrows at the boy.

Deeper and deeper into the cave they went.

"Can you believe that people hid in this cave? It's so cold in here. OUCH!" Kaya cried.

"What happened?" asked Carlos.

"I kicked something," she answered.

"It wasn't a skeleton, was it?" AJ asked fearfully.

"No, it feels like a chain," Kaya answered as she bent over to examine the object.

"Pick it up," said Nikki.

"Yep, that's what it is, a chain," said Kaya.

"Give it to me. I'll protect us with it in case something comes after us," said Carlos as he traded it with his flashlight.

"I really think we should go back now," AJ pleaded. "We've seen a lot—can we go?"

They all agreed they'd had enough

and headed back toward the entrance of the cave, Carlos swinging the chain as he walked.

"I can smell burgers on the grill!" announced the ever-hungry AJ as they stepped into the sun.

The kids walked over to Papa Lemon and found him hard at work over the barbecue. Nikki excitedly told him that they had gone into the cave and looked around.

"Did you see any skeletons?" Papa Lemon asked.

"No," Carlos said.

Mama Sarah called out, "The food is done—you can eat now!" The kids scurried to pile their plates with burgers and hotdogs. After they ate, everyone went to play softball. Soon the sun began to set; the cars were packed and the families returned home.

The next day the kids went to Papa Lemon's house. Carlos had the chain they had found in the cave. "Where did you get that chain?" Papa Lemon asked Carlos as the kids approached the porch.

"We found it in the cave yesterday," he answered.

"Do you know what that chain was used for?" inquired Papa Lemon. The kids shrugged

and said they did not know.

"Well, chains just like that were used to try to keep slaves from running away from their slave masters." The kids looked at Papa Lemon, shock covering their faces. Papa Lemon reminded the kids of the story of the cave they had been in—how slaves hid there waiting to go North to be free. Carlos dropped the chain.

"How were they going to get to freedom?" asked Nikki.

"They used the underground railroad," continued Papa Lemon.

"What's that?" asked AJ.

"That was one way the slaves escaped. They were helped by a woman named Harriet Tubman," the wise man replied. "She helped many slaves escape by hiding them in caves, barns, crates, whatever she could find. She did not do it alone, though. She had help from the abolitionists who also thaught slavery was wrong. It was very dangerous, but they did it."

"Was your father a slave, Papa Lemon?" asked Nikki.

"No," he answered. "Slavery was over when he was born, but my grandpa was. I never got a chance to know him."

"Let's go back to that time for just a quick minute," Baby Buck said, half asking.

"I don't want to be a slave!" AJ cried nervously.

"Don't you want to see how our great great grandparents lived?" Nikki inquired. "We won't have to stay long."

Papa Lemon said thoughtfully, "You'd have to be very careful. It will be a dangerous trip. Are you sure you want to do this?" Papa Lemon looked hesitant, but the kids nodded with determination.

"Okay, you kids know how to get to your adventure."

They went to the attic and found some tattered old clothes. The boys used rope to hold up their pants while the girls found dresses and scarves to tie around their heads. Mama Sarah tried to talk them out of this adventure as she watched them choose their

clothes. "It's too dangerous. You kids pick
another adventure."

"We promise to be careful. We just want
to see for ourselves what it was like," said
Nikki. "PLEASE?"

Mama Sarah tweaked Nikki's nose. "Okay."

AJ set the dial to 1852 and Baby Buck
reminded Carlos that it was his turn to pull

the gearshift. Carlos stepped back and Baby
Buck eagerly put his hand on the lever. Kaya
reminded Baby Buck that he did not have to
pull too hard.

"And wait until we are all ready!" Nikki
added. "Before we go, let's make sure we
stick together. We don't want to get caught and
split up."

"Or worse, get sold as slaves," AJ said
nervously.

Carlos tried to comfort everyone by telling
them he would protect them. "Now let's do this
before we all chicken out."

"You kids be careful," Papa Lemon said
nervously.

They shouted, "We will!"

With those final words, Papa Lemon
stepped off the train, removing his hat and
wiping the sweat off his forehead with his
handkerchief.

Baby Buck pulled on the lever and the train
began to shake and rattle as it began the trip
back through time.

The Little Wanderers found themselves in
a cave, and as they walked out into the sunlight,

they saw Harriet Tubman. She was motioning wildly, telling them, "Hurry! The slave catchers are coming! Don't you want to get to freedom?"

Before they could reply, Harriet ran ahead to help a pregnant woman. Kaya squinted at the pregnant woman, trying to get a better look at her. Something about her looked familiar. She nudged Nikki. "Do we know her?" she asked, nodding toward the woman.

"That's impossible! This is the year 1852—

there's no way we could know her," responded Nikki. Kaya shrugged but couldn't help feeling like she'd seen the woman before. She was watching the woman so intently that Kaya didn't immediately see the net come down over their heads. The terrified kids began calling out, "Mama Sarah! Papa Lemon!"

The slave catcher shouted out, "No one

can help you kids now! You are all mine and I'm gonna sell all of you!" The man quickly chained the kids' feet together and herded them into a wagon.

"What are we going to do now?" cried AJ. "How are we going to get home? I'm scared." His voice trailed off as he bit his lip nervously.

Nikki grabbed his hand and comforted him. "We're going to be okay," she said, her voice trembling with uncertainty.

Kaya looked at Carlos. "I had a bad feeling about this! I wish we had stayed home."

AJ asked the question no one wanted to ask out loud. "What if we don't get sold together? How will we get back to the cave? How will we get home?"

"Calm down, AJ," Carlos whispered. "We have to watch the road so we can find our way back to the cave. Baby Buck, keep your eyes open—try to remember the trees and the swamp over there. We will get back!"

The slave catcher made his way to the slave auction. When they arrived at the auction,

he could be heard bragging to a buddy about how much money he should get for the kids. "Yep," he sneered, "I got myself a good catch here." He spit out a mouthful of tobacco. "I reckon I will get near a thousand dollars with these five kids."

Kaya asked the popular question. "How are we going to get back home?"

Nikki attempted to calm her, "All we have to do is get back to the cave. We are not that far from it. Maybe when somebody buys us, we will go by the cave and we can jump out, run to the opening and take the train home."

The kids were thrown into a pen with the other slaves. The auction began shortly after they arrived. The Little Wanderers stuck together hoping to be sold as a group. Together they watched in disbelief as the slaves were put on the auction block with chains around their ankles. All the slaves were lined up so they could be examined. Slave masters were checking their teeth and looking in their hair. The prospective buyers looked carefully at the slaves' muscles and looked them over for any lash marks. Obedient slaves didn't have scars from a whip. It was like they were looking at animals.

The Little Wanderers were sold within minutes, but Carlos, Kaya and AJ were unchained from the rest of the group and lead to

a wagon. Kaya screamed and reached for Nikki. "No! No! Please don't take me away!" she cried.

Carlos and AJ tried to tell her that she'd be okay. "Look, that other guy has Nikki and Baby Buck and he's talking to the man that bought us."

The kids listened as the two slave masters talked. "Well, it looks like we both got good deals today. Maybe sometime we can exchange our slaves or you can lend yours to me. I have a big crop this year and I can't afford to buy any more slaves. I will pay you, of course."

"Come by and we'll talk more about it," said the other owner.

Nikki turned to Baby Buck. "We have a chance—the owners are neighbors. Maybe we will be able to sneak out tomorrow night." Another slave heard their conversation and told them to keep quiet.

They reached the slave master's house, and their new owner told the slave who drove the wagon to take the kids to the barn and teach them the rules. The slave led the kids into the barn and instructed them never to speak aloud while the master was around. "You will be whipped. And what's this talk of running away? Don't you know what happens if you get caught trying to run away?" he said.

The kids shook their heads.

"If you try to run away and you get caught, you could be whipped, burned or even killed!"

Nikki began to cry.

"We don't belong here! We have to try to go home," Baby Buck said, as a wide-eyed Nikki sobbed softly behind him.

"Don't you understand, boy? You belong to the master! You two had best get that into your heads. You are here to stay!

"Now you kids, wait here. I have to go to the big house where the master lives. I will bring you back something to eat. Don't talk to anyone about running away; it's a dangerous idea. Try and get some rest; you're going to need it. Tomorrow you will be working in the field picking cotton."

"Picking cotton? I don't know how to pick cotton!" Nikki said while pacing back and forth.

Baby Buck rubbed his eyes. "This has got to be a dream. I can't believe this is happening."

Less than a mile away Kaya, Carlos and AJ tried to deal with the same dilemma as they sat in their master's barn. They went up to the hayloft and sat in a circle.

"What's happening?" Kaya cried.

"Everything was going so fast, we couldn't stick

to the plan. How are we going to get out of this mess? Carlos, you told us you would take care of us! What are you going to do?"

AJ bravely spoke up, "It's not Carlos's fault we got caught!"

Carlos lay back in the hay, thinking about what he needed to do to get the gang out of trouble. He remembered seeing a blacksmith talking to the master about shoeing some horses as they got off the wagon. The blacksmith had given him a wink and the tiniest of nods when he saw Carlos listening in. Something in the blacksmith's look brought out the special courage in Carlos and he decided the blacksmith could be trusted. He thought he would risk everything and tell the blacksmith about escaping. "I've got it!" he said, springing to his feet. "You two stay here. I'm going to check something out."

"Don't leave! We should stay together," Kaya quietly called out.

"No, you two stay here," Carlos said as he climbed down the ladder and out of the hayloft.

AJ leaned over the edge of the loft. "Try to bring back something to eat," he said.

Carlos snuck outside and made his way toward a nearby shed where the blacksmith was pounding a red-hot horseshoe.

"What are you doing here?" the blacksmith asked. "If the boss man catches you, trouble will soon follow."

"I was careful. I need to get my friends and me out of here and fast."

"You're not going anywhere," the blacksmith said. He paused. "Not alone. I'm Jesse," said the blacksmith with another friendly wink. He told Carlos to close the door and began to tell him about how Harriet Tubman was coming to help slave families escape from farms in the area. "Harriet Tubman is a great woman who helps slaves like us escape. Day or night she will save us, the stars leading us through the night. She has never lost a slave on a journey. Ms. Tubman is very brave and she expects us to be brave, too. If a slave gets too scared and wants to go back, she will use the gun she always carries to make them keep going. She uses that gun to protect slaves from other people and from themselves. If one person went back, they would put everyone at risk of being caught."

"How will we know when she's here? What do we need to do?" asked Carlos.

"I will give you the sign. Just trust me. I'm putting new shoes on the two fastest horses so they can take us away. There's enough room in the wagon for ten people. How many people will be coming with you?" Jesse asked.

"There're five of us," Carlos answered, "three here and two at the other farm."

"I'm building a false floor in this wagon. You and your friends will be able to lie on your backs underneath it without the boss man knowing you're in the wagon."

"That's smart thinking," Carlos said.

"Make sure you and your friends stay close together while you work in the fields picking sweet potatoes tomorrow."

"How do you know we will be in the fields?" Carlos asked.

"That's why the master bought you and your friends. There's a big crop and he needs more help to pick the potatoes before they rot in the ground.

"The master will be going into town tomorrow afternoon. When I bring the water bucket to the field, I want you and your friends to climb into the wagon with the others and hang on with all your might because we're going to ride to freedom! We can make only one stop to pick up your friends at the other farm where they will be picking cotton by the roadside. Last week I was at the other farm making some new tools. While I was there, I told those slaves to get ready to ride to freedom. They'll be ready for us. Harriet Tubman will be waiting to meet us in the woods, so we can't stop again once we get going."

"How did you tell them that Harriet Tubman was coming? Wasn't the master around to hear you?" Carlos asked.

Jesse chuckled and shook his head. "Oh, he was around alright, but he doesn't know our songs. Our songs have secret messages in them so we can tell each other about escaping without the boss man knowing. Tonight you'll hear some of us singing 'Git on Board, Little Chillen'. That song lets other slaves know that a lot of people will run away tomorrow. There's a lot of meaning in the songs we sing; you just have to know what to listen for."

Jesse got up and took some bread out of a cupboard in the corner. "Now, take some of this food for you and your friends and get some sleep. Be ready for tomorrow because freedom is coming." With those words, Jesse handed

Carlos the dark brown bread and sent him back to the hayloft.

Back in the barn, AJ was trying to comfort Kaya when Carlos returned. "Hey, you guys, I found a way for us to get out of here and get back to the train," Carlos whispered loudly. He handed out the food and told them the plan for the next day.

Feeling somewhat relieved at the prospect of returning home soon, Kaya told AJ what she had planned for her arrival back home. "I'm going to go to my room and clean it really well. I'll do whatever my mom tells me to do. I just want to get home!"

AJ agreed. "I can't wait to tell Papa Lemon about all of this. I miss him," he said sadly.

None of the kids could sleep, thinking of what the next day would bring. Their thoughts turned to all the slaves before them, how they died trying to get to freedom. They couldn't help but think of what would happen to them if they were caught.

The next morning, the slave masters at

both farms yelled out instructions to their slaves.

"Get out there and pick that cotton! I don't want to see any dirt mixed in!"

"Get to picking those potatoes so we can sell all we've got!"

Working the fields in the hot sun was hard work. "I don't think I can make it," Nikki said to Baby Buck.

An older lady overheard Nikki. "Baby, come over here and let me help you." She dunked a towel into a bucket of water and placed it on Nikki's head. The lady also gave her a big hat to keep the sun off. "Now you go on, baby. This will help a lot."

Nikki thanked her. "How long have you been here?" she asked.

"Child, I've been here since I was your age. I was lucky. I always had my mom and dad until they went on to Glory ten years ago. Now they are buried over yonder. Some of my friends weren't as lucky—their families were split up when someone was sold away.

"You and your friend go over to my

children by the road. They will help you and
make it easy for you on your first day."

The woman looked around. Many of the
slaves nearby were singing, "Steal away, steal
away, steal away to Jesus! Steal away, steal away
home, I ain't got long to stay here."

As the old lady placed the hat on Nikki's
head, she told her to watch for the sign to
escape. "Work next to my children and get as
close to the road as you can. There's a wagon

to freedom coming soon. When you see that wagon coming, you and your friend drop those sacks, run as fast as you can and jump on that wagon. God be with you, child," she said with a worried smile.

Nikki thanked the woman and went to tell Baby Buck the instructions the old lady had given her. Together they went to find the old woman's children and get into position by the road.

As Nikki and Baby Buck picked the cotton, they found it was not as easy as it looked. They kept getting their fingers pricked by the husks that surrounded the fluffy white cotton. "How do they do it?" a sweaty Nikki asked as she sucked on her sore fingers. She hoped her friends were having an easier time at the other farm.

A few miles away, Carlos, Kaya, and AJ were having a hard time with the potatoes they were picking and putting into sacks tied around their waists. Kaya complained about all the dirt that was getting under her nails and AJ was sneaking bites of the potatoes as he pulled them

from the ground. Carlos was keeping pace with
the others while he watched for the wagon to
come around. Carlos instructed Kaya and AJ
to stand close to the other slaves so it would
be harder for the master to see them get on
the wagon.

As the kids moved to join a group of slaves
at the edge of the field, the slave master went to
get his horse and buggy to go to town. "Get the
field hands some water," the boss man called to

Jesse. That was music to the children's ears. It was almost time to go! Jesse gave a tiny nod to the Little Wanderers and went to the barn where the wagon was hooked up to the fastest horses and the old broken-down mule was hooked up to the master's buggy.

Carlos nudged AJ and Kaya closer to the road. The boss man had not yet noticed that Jesse had taken the good horses, but they didn't have much time before he would catch on. Jesse quickly brought the wagon to where the kids were standing with a group of other slaves by the road. Carlos jumped into the wagon, grabbed Kaya by the hand and lifted her up. Together they reached down to pull AJ aboard. Jesse had already lifted three planks off the false floor so the kids could slide underneath the remaining planks and escape unseen. A couple of field hands jumped in and put the planks back over the children so they were hidden.

Just as the children were being covered by the last plank, the boss man noticed that the two best horses were hitched to the wagon and

yelled out to Jesse, "What are you doing with my best horses? Get them back in the barn and I mean now!"

Jesse told everyone to hold on with all their might. "It's time to go. Yaahh!" He cracked his whip at the horses and off they went through the fields heading for the next farm to pick up Nikki and Baby Buck.

The wagon took off across the bumpy field. Three of the planks flew off the wagon and Carlos sat up quickly to look around. He leaned over the side of the wagon and looked behind to make sure the slave master wasn't following them. As he leaned over, the wagon hit a bump and Carlos started to fall toward the ground, only to be saved by a nail sticking out from the back of the wagon. Kaya cried out, "AJ, grab him!"

As AJ reached out for Carlos, another slave pulled him back. Carlos dangled helplessly by the nail, his head inches from the ground. A hand reached down and grabbed Carlos by the waist and pulled him back into the wagon. To his surprise, it was a woman who pulled him to safety. She told him, "Hang on! We're going to make it. Look yonder—there're your friends."

As the wagon got closer to the second farm, Nikki and Baby Buck dropped their sacks

and, with two other slaves, ran as fast as they could and jumped onto the wagon. Kaya grabbed Nikki and held her tightly. "I missed you! I was so scared! Are we going to make it? Are we going to make it back to Papa

Lemon?"

The Little Wanderers looked up and saw
that the slave catchers were hot on their trail.
The wagon raced around the curves of the dusty
road on two wheels, and the kids screamed for
their lives. Soon they got to the swamp and they
knew they were near the cave. Nikki looked up,
"I see it! I see the cave! We are going to have
to jump off. Get ready!" All the kids crouched
at the edge of the wagon and waited for Nikki's
instructions. "Jump!" she shouted, as the wagon

rounded another corner.

The kids leaped and landed a short distance from the cave. A few of the slave catchers had already jumped off the other wagon and were right behind them. "Come back here! You will be whipped for trying to run away. We'll chain you up and make sure you don't try it again!"

The kids sprinted into the cave following Carlos's lead. "Do you remember which way?" Kaya asked, running along side Carlos.

"Yes," he said breathlessly. "I hear them getting closer—hurry!"

The kids reached the train and hopped on, the slave catchers on their heels. "Hold on," Carlos said, his hand on the gearshift. He gave the gearshift a pull and in a flash, the kids were back in Papa Lemon's shed.

Papa Lemon had been waiting anxiously for their return and ran over to the train as soon as he saw the kids.

"Oh, Papa Lemon, we never want to go back to that time ever again! It was horrible! We had to work so hard in the hot sun, and we could not even drink water when we wanted to or talk when we wanted to. We had to sleep in a barn and use hay for a bed, and there were bugs all over the place. We all agreed that when we got home we would clean our rooms and whatever else our parents ask. That's a piece of cake compared to what we had to do as slaves," Nikki said breathlessly as the words tumbled out of her.

Papa Lemon took his handkerchief and wiped the dirt off Kaya's face, and Mama Sarah came out with a tray of lemonade and cookies in her hands and tears of joy in her eyes. "Come here," she said. She put her arms around all of them and kissed their heads. "I was so worried! You kids, come inside and get cleaned up, and I will tell you about how my grandparents lived as slaves and how they ran away from their master. I've even got some pictures of them after they escaped."

The exhausted Little Wanderers followed Mama Sarah into the house and sat down on the soft couch in the living room while she retrieved a huge photo album from the bookshelf. Mama Sarah paged through the photos, passing pictures of the neighborhood kids playing on the farm and pictures of her and Papa Lemon, their friends and their family. At the end of the book were some very old black and white photographs. "These are all the slaves that escaped with my grandparents. They all worked on a farm together. These two are my grandparents," said Mama Sarah, pointing to two people standing together. Mama

Sarah's grandmother was holding a tiny baby in her arms.

Kaya gasped. "We saw that woman when we first got off the train! She was running with Harriet Tubman and she was pregnant!"

The kids saw tears in Mama Sarah's eyes. "That baby is my mother. She was born the night that my grandparents ran away. She was the first baby in our family to be born free."

The kids stared at the photo for a long time. Mama Sarah had her grandmother's warm eyes and bright smile. As they looked through the rest of the photos, they could see all of the people they cared about smiling back at them. "I can't wait until we can put Aunt Kay's picture in here," Baby Buck said smiling at his friends.

Everyone nodded in agreement.